The Adventures of AUSSIE AND OTIS

Summer
Vacation

by R.P. Huttinga

Illustrations by Kurt Hershey

Mrs. B woke up early and put on her yellow slippers. She tiptoed softly down the old, squeaky wooden floor. On her way to the laundry room, she stopped and looked out the hallway window, smiling as she watched the bees buzzing around her flower garden. The July breeze made the large maple leaves dance in the wind.

PERFECT, she thought, as she gathered the laundry from the washing machine. She placed it in the basket and quietly went outside to the clothesline by the maple trees.

Aussie was still asleep, as the warm breeze entered through the kitchen windows, gently touching her old body. She slowly lifted her head and smiled, knowing that Mrs. B would soon be changing her bedding with a fresh blanket and two fluffy pillows.

Otis was still asleep when the smell of pancakes filled the room. He took a deep breath, smacked his lips, and smiled. Saturday morning was his favourite day of the week. Mrs. B would always leave him the last piece of pancake, covered in maple syrup.

After breakfast, Mrs. B went into the garage and got two big coolers and some empty boxes, brought them into the kitchen, and placed them on the counter.

"Well, I have a surprise for you two," she said to Otis and Aussie. "We're going on holidays today."

Otis had a puzzled look on his face.

"Are we were moving?" he asked Aussie.

"Oh no," Aussie said. "Mrs. B rents a cabin in the mountains every year. I heard her tell Mr. Wilson that the cabin was near Mt. Apps." Otis looked at Aussie and asked how far away the mountain was. "Oh, about three good naps for me."

OH NO, thought Otis. **THIS IS GOING TO BE FAR.** He knew how much Aussie loved to nap.

Mrs. B finished loading the old VW van as Otis watched from the window. "She sure has packed a lot of stuff, Aussie. I hope she remembers my favourite ball by the maple tree."

Mrs. B made sure she had all the boxes, then went inside to get Aussie and Otis. As they started down the driveway, Mrs. B placed her favourite CD into the radio and started to sing. Looking at Otis in the mirror, she asked if he would like to join her, and he started howling as Mrs. B laughed and started to sing again.

Aussie closed her eyes and fell asleep. They drove for many hours before reaching a logging road. "Hold on," she told the dogs. "It's going to be bumpy."

They drove for an hour until Mrs. B spotted the long driveway, with the yellow mailbox, which led to the cabin. As they drove towards the cabin, Aussie and Otis could see large trees and green valleys in the distance, with snow on the mountaintops.

Finally, they came to the cabin. Mrs. B stopped the van, opened the door, and let Aussie and Otis out. They both did a big stretch and look around. Otis lifted his head, trying to smell the mountain air.

"It looks just like the picture in the magazine I saw in the living room," Otis said to Aussie.

Mrs. B walked up the path and noticed a white porch swing, overlooking the meadow. She smiled, stepped up to the cabin, opened the door, and went inside. In the living room, she found a note attached to a yellow vase, which was full of

FRESH-CUT FLOWERS,

sitting on the fireplace mantle.

The note said, "Mrs. B, Aussie, and Otis, we hope you have a wonderful holiday." Smiling at the thoughtful message, Mrs. B started unloading the car, placing the boxes on the kitchen table.

Aussie was about to have a nap on the porch when Otis appeared. He was all excited, telling Aussie that he had found a secret trail behind the cabin. His little tail was wagging, and he asked her to join him on an adventure. Aussie stretched and agreed.

Together, they followed the trail until they heard the sound of running water close by. "Sounds like our stream back home," Otis said to Aussie.

They both walked around the bend and saw a large grizzly bear drinking from the stream. They both stopped in their tracks, as the grizzly bear looked up and started to growl.

Aussie quickly told Otis to stand underneath her. Little Otis did so and started shaking, as the bear came closer. Then the grizzly bear stopped growling and looked at Aussie, unable to believe her eyes.

"Aussie? Do you remember me?" she asked.

Aussie looked at the grizzly and blinked.

"DAKOTA?"

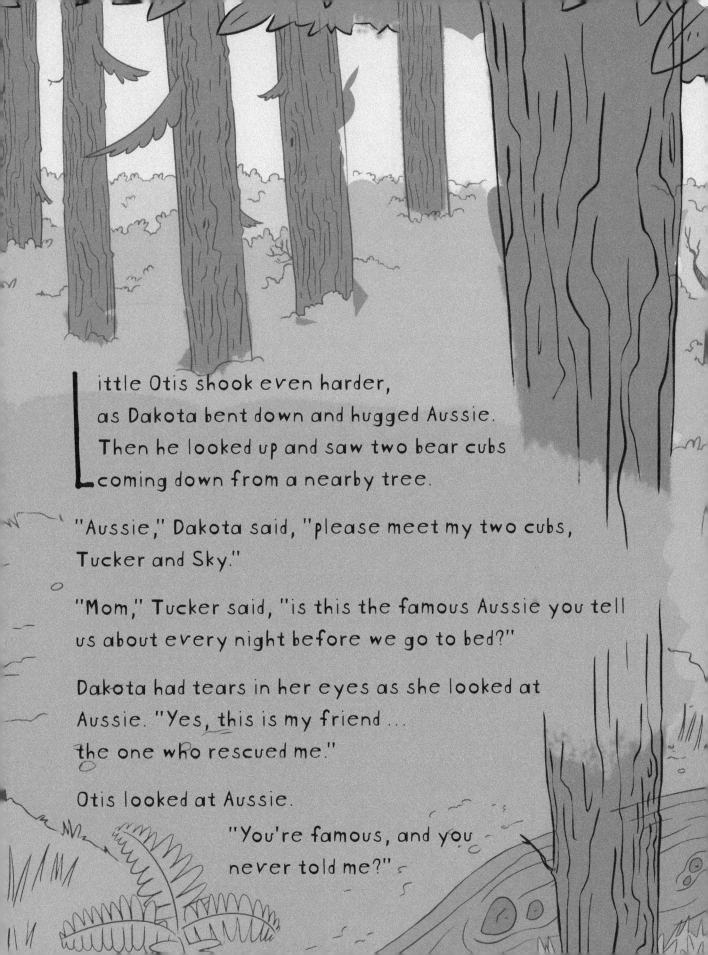

Little Otis shook even harder,
as Dakota bent down and hugged Aussie.
Then he looked up and saw two bear cubs
coming down from a nearby tree.

"Aussie," Dakota said, "please meet my two cubs,
Tucker and Sky."

"Mom," Tucker said, "is this the famous Aussie you tell
us about every night before we go to bed?"

Dakota had tears in her eyes as she looked at
Aussie. "Yes, this is my friend ...
the one who rescued me."

Otis looked at Aussie.

"You're famous, and you
never told me?"

Aussie smiled, as Dakota asked everyone to join them near the stream. Once there, Otis and the two cubs sat on a log, eagerly listening as Dakota started to tell the story of how their unusual friendship began.

"There was a late winter storm," she told them, "which brought a great amount of snow to the mountain, making the trails unpassable. Doc Peters was a very kind man who owned a cabin near Helena Lake. He helped injured and orphaned animals, and I was one of them.

"One windy night, while coming back from the barn, a large branch fell and injured Doc Peter's leg. Luckily, he was able to crawl back to his cabin and radio for help. I watched all this happen through the cracks in the barn door."

Otis's eyes were fixed on Aussie, and the cubs were grinning. They had heard this story before and always enjoyed it.

"When the news spread that Doc Peters was in trouble," she continued, "no one in town was brave enough to go out in the blizzard to bring help to him, except Aussie's sled-dog team. Aussie and her team were loaded up with supplies for Doc Peters and us animals, and they headed out. After two days, the dogs were all too tired to go any further, except for Aussie. She grabbed the sled and continued on the snowy trail. The snow and ice were stinging her face, but she continued on.

"FINALLY,

she saw a flickering light in the cabin window, glowing through the winter storm. She reached the back door and started to bark. Doc Peters slowly opened the door, using a fallen branch to help him stand, and looked at Aussie. 'I can't believe you made it here all by yourself,' he said, as he bent down and patted her.

"He put on his coat and boots and limped towards the barn with all the supplies Aussie had brought with her. Aussie could hear me crying in the barn, and followed Doc Peters inside, laying beside me and keeping me warm on those cold winter nights.

When the snow finally started to melt, we would go outside at night and watch the Northern Lights."

Dakota smiled at Aussie. "We became close friends."

"Is this all true?" Otis asked Aussie, looking at her.

"Every word," the cubs said together, with big grins on their faces.

"I never saw Aussie again," said Dakota, "until today at least, but the legend of Aussie spread throughout the mountain. Every animal knew what Aussie had done."

Aussie smiled, and was about to respond when they heard Mrs. B calling. "Well, we better go now," she told Otis.

They said goodbye to Dakota and her cubs, and as they were walking back to the cabin, they could see Mrs. B sitting on the porch swing, sipping a cup of tea.

"Well," she said, watching as Otis and Aussie approached, "looks like you two had quite an adventure today."

Aussie slowly walked up the porch stairs and laid down on her soft bed beside the porch swing. Otis followed her, with a smile on his face.

"Aussie," he said, cuddling up beside her, "could you tell me more of your amazing stories?"

Aussie grinned.

"I WILL, OTIS, ON OUR NEXT ADVENTURE."

THE
END

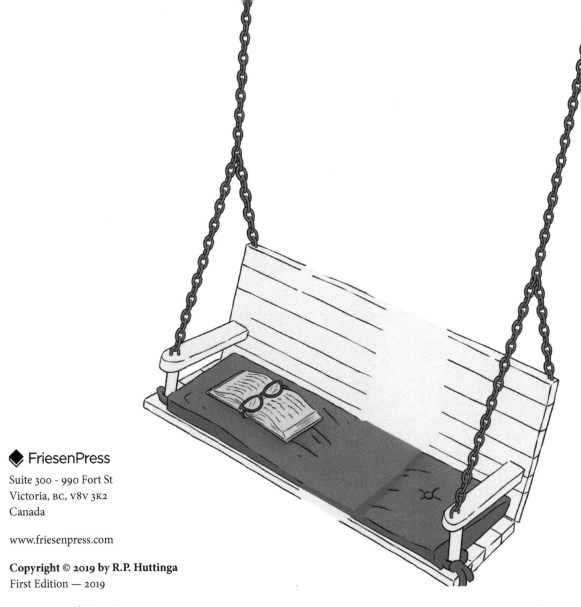

◆ FriesenPress

Suite 300 - 990 Fort St
Victoria, BC, V8V 3K2
Canada

www.friesenpress.com

ISBN
978-1-5255-5589-3 (Hardcover)
978-1-5255-5590-9 (Paperback)
978-1-5255-5591-6 (eBook)

1. JUVENILE FICTION, ANIMALS, DOGS

Distributed to the trade by The Ingram Book Company

In loving memory of Aussie
2000 - 2017

"LOOK FOR AUSSIE AND OTIS IN

"MOVING DAY"

CPSIA information can be obtained
at www.ICGtesting.com
Printed in the USA
LVHW012129101019
633848LV00001B/1/P